THE
BLUE SPRUCE

MARIO CUOMO

Illustrated by Gijsbert van Frankenhuyzen

SLEEPING BEAR PRESS

To Our Nine Jewels and Their Great Grandparents.

—Mario Cuomo

Sleeping Bear Press
121 South Main
P.O. Box 20
Chelsea, Michigan 48118
www.sleepingbearpress.com

Printed and bound in Canada by Friesens, Altona, Manitoba.
10 9 8 7 6 5 4 3 2 1

Cuomo, Mario Matthew.
The blue spruce / by Mario Cuomo; illustrated by Gijsbert van Frankenhuyzen.
p. cm.
Summary: When a storm knocks down the blue spruce tree in a boy's yard, he and his father work with all their might to
right the tree again.
ISBN 1-886947-76-7
[1. Trees Fiction. 2. Storms Fiction. 3. Fathers and sons Fiction.] I. Frankenhuyzen, Gijsbert van, ill. II. Title.
PZ7.C91745B1 1999
[E]—dc21
99-33431
CIP

I met the Blue Spruce a long time ago when I was a boy. I believed from the very beginning that it was more than just a beautiful tree.

In those days my imagination was livelier. I felt the great Spruce understood my words and thoughts and even tried to speak back to me. But I never heard the Spruce more clearly than I did years later when I was fully grown, in a tough political race for Governor, far behind and discouraged. A chance glimpse at an old business card describing my Father's small grocery store, reminded me of a day in the life of the great tree that I will never forget again. It was a recollection that gave me the inspiration I needed to overcome my timidity and go on to be Governor of the great State of New York.

Listen to the Blue Spruce, and to Papa: they can do the same for you.

—Mario Cuomo

It was late afternoon, just before dinner,
when Papa told me that we were moving.
The streets were busy with people and cars.
The buildings were tall and full of noise.

Papa said that we didn't need to
live in the small apartment behind
our family store anymore.

I felt sad inside.

Leaving the rooms behind
our grocery store would mean
a lot of changes.

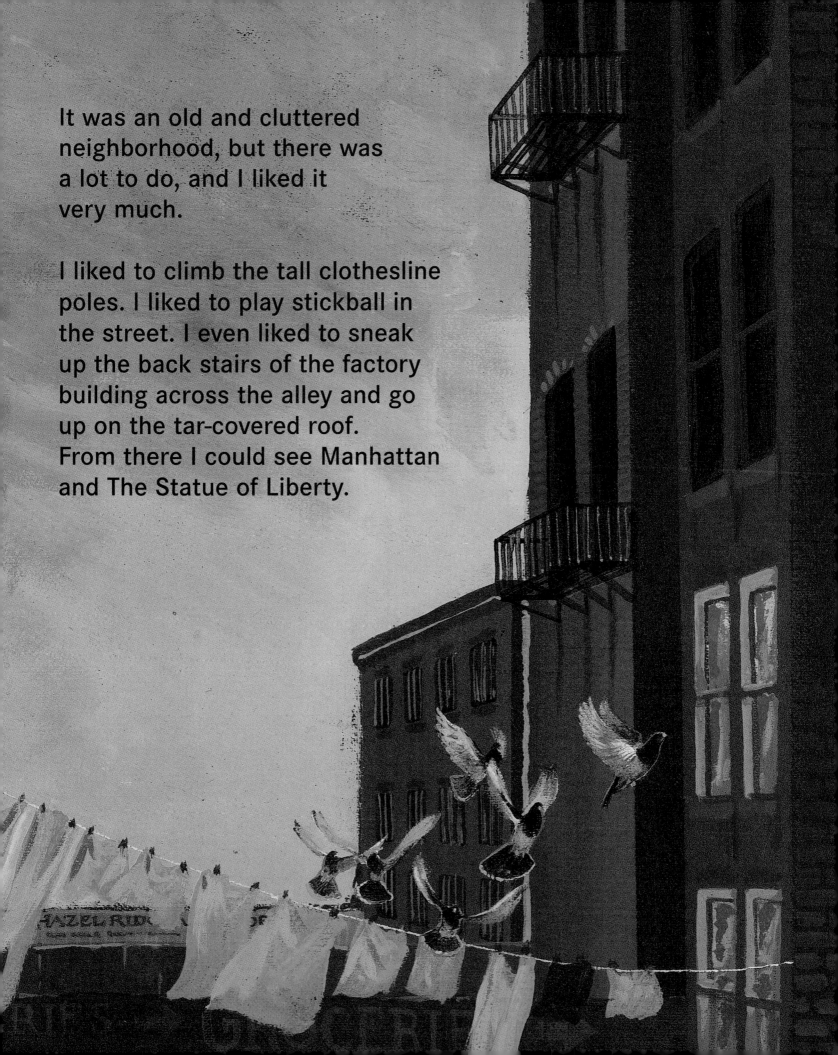

It was an old and cluttered
neighborhood, but there was
a lot to do, and I liked it
very much.

I liked to climb the tall clothesline
poles. I liked to play stickball in
the street. I even liked to sneak
up the back stairs of the factory
building across the alley and go
up on the tar-covered roof.
From there I could see Manhattan
and The Statue of Liberty.

But Papa said the new
place would be different.
He said our new home
wouldn't be part of a building
with a lot of other families in it.
Instead, it would be a house
with a yard to play in and a
great big beautiful tree with
branches that spread out
into the sky.

Papa told me that having a house with a yard and a tree to call our own was his very special dream. He said, "I've worked hard and waited for a very long time to share it with you."

And then he said, "That's how it is when you have a dream. You work and you wait, you never give up."

I thought Papa's dream sounded like a good dream to have.

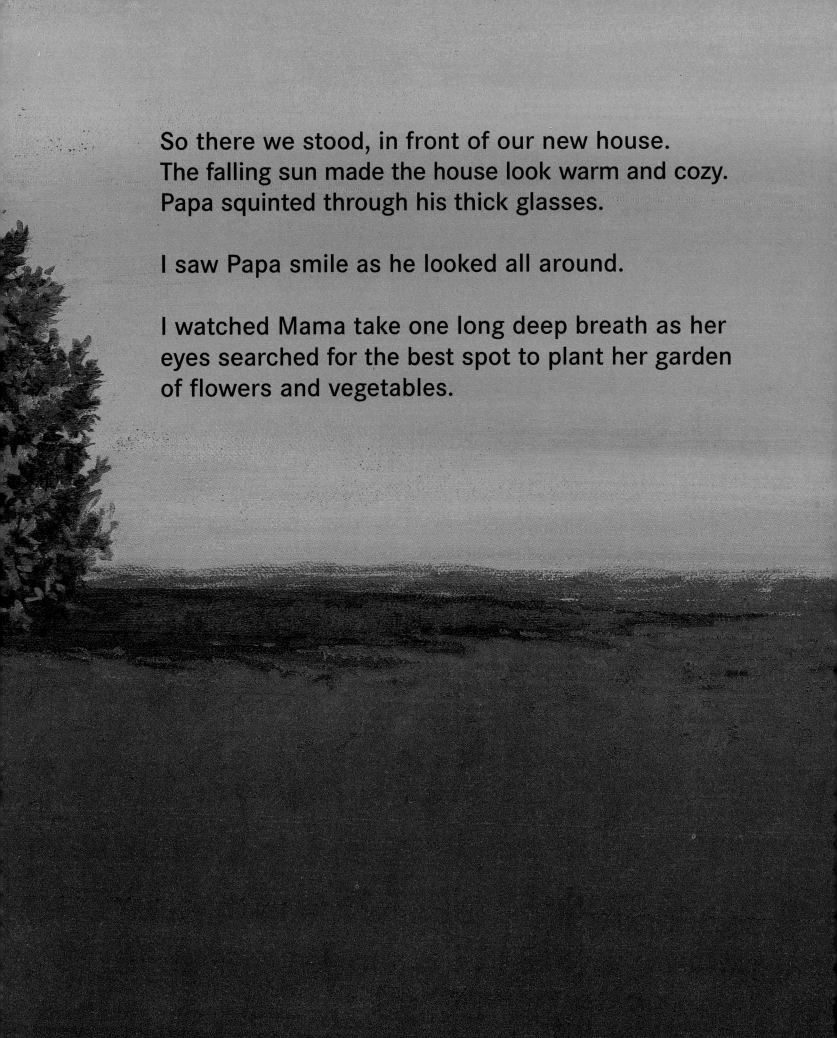

So there we stood, in front of our new house.
The falling sun made the house look warm and cozy.
Papa squinted through his thick glasses.

I saw Papa smile as he looked all around.

I watched Mama take one long deep breath as her
eyes searched for the best spot to plant her garden
of flowers and vegetables.

Papa took me by the hand and led me to the shadow of a very large tree. We were so close together that I could hear Papa breathing. The tree was full of blue-gray needles and it made the air around us smell sweet and spicy.

Then Papa said to me,
"This is a Blue Spruce
and it is ours."

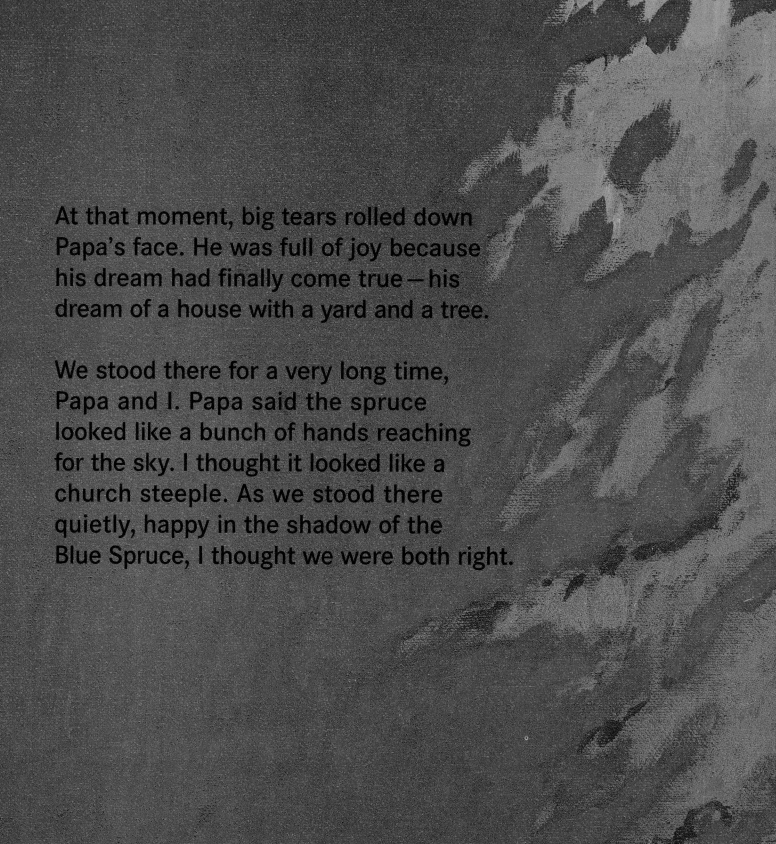

At that moment, big tears rolled down Papa's face. He was full of joy because his dream had finally come true—his dream of a house with a yard and a tree.

We stood there for a very long time, Papa and I. Papa said the spruce looked like a bunch of hands reaching for the sky. I thought it looked like a church steeple. As we stood there quietly, happy in the shadow of the Blue Spruce, I thought we were both right.

We quickly became friends,
the Blue Spruce and I.

I read books beside it
on warm summer days.

I made snowmen near it in the winter. I liked how the Blue Spruce would guard and protect them from blowing over during cold and blustery winter nights.

In the spring, I liked to find patterns
in the mix of twigs, and to watch
as the new, greener coat would grow,
right over the needles that were the newest
and greenest the year before.

And sometimes, I'd stand in its shadow
for no reason at all.

Sometimes, Papa would join me, and there
we would be, saying nothing at all about life
or dreams or trees. It was just Papa and me,
in the shadow of the Blue Spruce.

Sometimes at night, I would rest my chi
upon my bedroom windowsill and whispe
great things to the Blue Spruce—stories tha
only a magnificent tree would understand

And when I was certain that the wind ha
carried my secrets to the tree, I would no
goodnight, and imagine the Blue Spruc
nodding its crown in retur

I believed the Blue Spruce understood wh
Papa had worked so hard and waited so lon
for his house with a yard and a tree

I believed the Blue Spruce knew
about Papa's dream

Late one afternoon when Papa and I were returning
home from the store, dark clouds rolled through
the sky and thunder exploded from all around.

Flashes of lightning popped back and forth,
lighting up the sky from every direction.

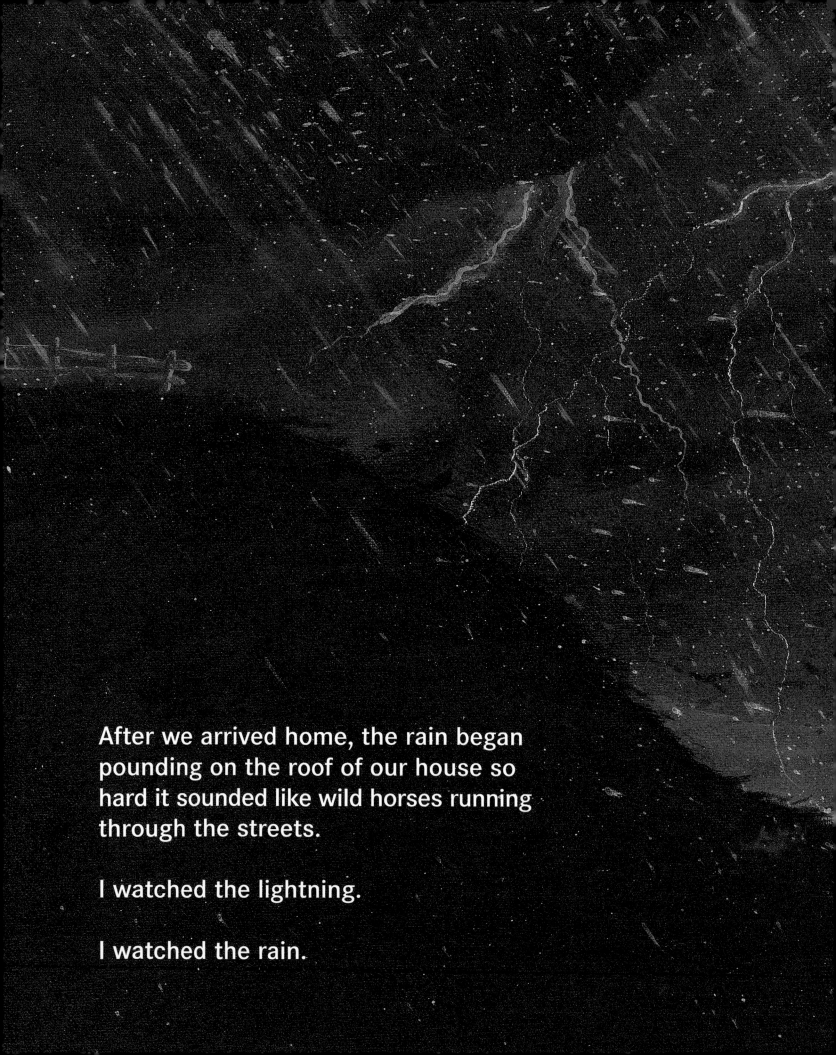

After we arrived home, the rain began
pounding on the roof of our house so
hard it sounded like wild horses running
through the streets.

I watched the lightning.

I watched the rain.

And I watched the Blue Spruce
fighting against the raging wind.

The earth at the base of the Blue Spruce
was soaked by the rain.

Low and terrible groans broke from the ground
as the wind kept pushing against the tree.

Snap! Crack!

Boom!

I saw the tree I loved so much
lying on its side. It looked weak and helpless.
Its limbs were broken and tangled.

I saw its gigantic roots whipping wildly about in the cold wind. They flew back and forth in the rain, begging to be put back in the dark, rich earth where they belonged.

My heart sank like a stone in a pond.

I followed Papa as he raced outside. I could not tell if it was the sharp rain hitting my face or the sadness in my heart that hurt so bad.

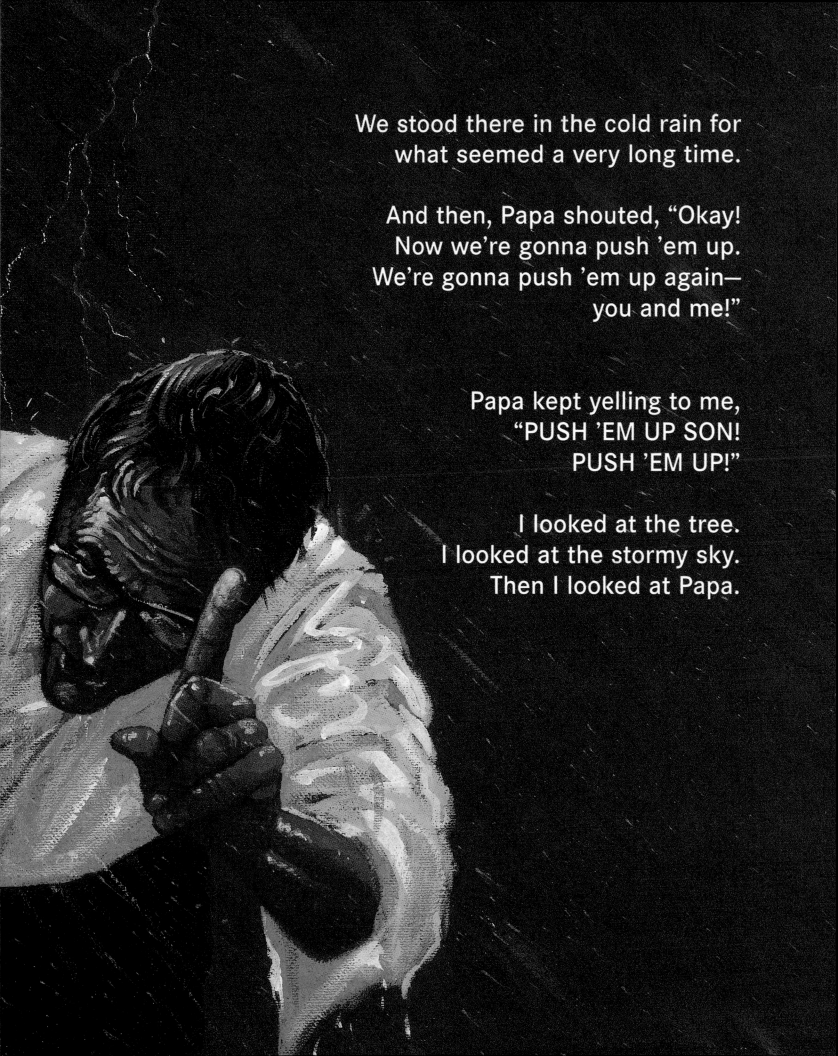

We stood there in the cold rain for
what seemed a very long time.

And then, Papa shouted, "Okay!
Now we're gonna push 'em up.
We're gonna push 'em up again—
you and me!"

Papa kept yelling to me,
"PUSH 'EM UP SON!
PUSH 'EM UP!"

I looked at the tree.
I looked at the stormy sky.
Then I looked at Papa.

There was no way a tree like that could ever be pushed up. There was no way those huge roots could be pushed back into the ground to grow once more. There was no way the Blue Spruce would ever be right again.

I turned away from Papa. I wanted to tell Papa that I did not believe him.

I wanted to tell him that I was wet and cold and mad. I wanted to tell him that he never should have gotten a house with a yard and a tree.

I wanted to tell Papa that I didn't believe in his dream anymore.

But just then a great flash of lightning
struck the ground. It lit Papa's face and
the huge tree at his feet.

I looked at Papa and saw the way his eyes
and lips looked in the cold hard rain and
I remembered how much the Blue Spruce
meant to him.

And then I realized how much it meant
to me, too. At that moment, I remembered
what Papa said about dreams.

"You work and you wait."

"You never give up."

So I raced back to Papa and the tree.

We pulled and we pushed.

We tugged and we heaved.

I pressed my body into the bark of
the trunk and tried to push the tree
with all of my might. The points of
the wet needles scratched my face.
The sharp edges of the broken
branches poked me.

Neither of us was saying
a word about the storm,
or about the Blue Spruce,
or about dreams.

I felt the roots ease
slightly toward the huge
hole in the ground.

I looked at Papa and
gave him a big smile.

Papa climbed the small hill in our yard, pulling on the rope he had tied near the top of the tree, while I pushed on its trunk.

Then Papa held the rope tightly while I pushed the muddy earth around the tree's roots.

I pushed and pounded the soil firmly into place,
pressing the roots inward to the world, where they belonged.

Then Papa rolled huge rocks toward the base of the tree so
that it wouldn't fall over.

I was working so hard that I didn't even notice
that the storm was over until I felt Papa's hand
on my shoulder. He told me not to worry,
that the Blue Spruce would grow again.

I noticed how the raindrops that pelted the tree
before were now clinging to each needle,
holding the evening sunlight as tiny balls of color.

Right then I understood what Papa meant.
I understood about his dream. I understood
about never giving up. I understood about
the Blue Spruce.

And as the evening sun fell,
we stood there for a long time, Papa and me,
quietly holding onto our dream and smiling,
happy once again in the shadow of the
beautiful Blue Spruce.

Governor Mario M. Cuomo

Mario Cuomo began life in the struggling neighborhood of South Jamaica, Queens, at the height of the Great Depression. He was the son of Andrea and Immaculata Cuomo, recent immigrants from rural Italy. Though he could barely speak English when he began first grade in the New York City public schools, Cuomo graduated summa cum laude in 1953 from St. John's University and in 1956 tied for top-of-the-class honors at St. John's University School of Law. He later served there for thirteen years as an adjunct professor of law.

Watching his parents struggle against all the odds, refusing ever to quit and seldom complaining, Mario Cuomo became convinced that "The game is lost only when we stop trying."—It has worked for him.

For nearly two decades, he fought as a lawyer for the ordinary citizen and eventually gained prominent public notice in 1972 when, at the request of New York City Mayor John Lindsay, he stepped in to resolve a bitter dispute over proposed public housing in the community of Forest Hills, Queens.

Cuomo continued to practice law unil 1975 when he was appointed by Governor Hugh Carey as New York's Secretary of State. In 1978 he was elected as Lieutenant Governor, a position he held until going on to win the governorship himself in 1982. He served 3 terms, 12 years, as the distinguished Governor of New York. Following his governorship, Cuomo returned to private practice and continues to practice law today in the New York firm of Willkie Farr & Gallagher. He has authored four books: *Forest Hills Diary, The Diaries of Mario Cuomo, The New York Idea,* and *Reason to Believe,* and has edited several other published works.

Married since 1954, the former governor and the former first lady, Matilda Raffa Cuomo, are the parents of five children: Margaret I. Cuomo, MD, married to Howard Maier; Andrew Cuomo, married to Kerry Kennedy; Maria Cuomo, married to Kenneth Cole; Madeline Cuomo, married to Brian O'Donoghue; and Christopher Cuomo. The Cuomos have nine granddaughters, and are trying to teach all of them "The game is lost only when we stop trying."

Gijsbert van Frankenhuyzen

One of Gijsbert's favorite places in this world is on his 27-acre farm in rural Bath, Michigan, where he lives with his wife Robbyn and his two teenage daughters, Heather and Kelly.

Gijsbert (also known as "Nick") made two new friends during the creation of The Blue Spruce—Jeff Baldori, musician extraordinare and model for Papa Cuomo, and Josh Stonehouse, a great kid who was the model for young Mario Cuomo. He appreciates the role playing they both had to do to make his paintings possible.

Gijsbert is the illustrator of two other children's books, *The Legend of Sleeping Bear,* which was designated Michigan's Official State Children's Book, and *The Legend of Mackinac Island.*